AF348083

E
Evincepub
Publishing

Evincepub Publishing

Parijat Extension, Bilaspur, Chhattisgarh

First Published by Evincepub Publishing 2020
Copyright © Koyel Mitra 2020
All Rights Reserved.
ISBN: 9789390442478

A Poet's Nook

By

Koyel Mitra

About the Book

Poetry is the music of the soul. The tunes of it often strike a chord with sensitive people. The words of these poems will surely resonate with you. These will immerse you in a variety of emotions. Sometimes you will feel happy. Sometimes you will feel sad. These will definitely succeed to empathize with your feelings.

ABOUT THE AUTHOR

Koyel Mitra has done Masters in Mathematics and teaches Mathematics at a government-aided high school. At the age of nine, she started writing and penned a mystery story. She has been writing poems since long and has been awarded prize at international poetry competition. She enjoys the position of a Preferred Author at www.writing.com. She resides in Kolkata and her hobbies include singing, reading books, sketching and writing.

Contents

1. *Sentinels of Night*

Having a sleepless night happened
To be a boon for me as
I could serve a sole testimony
To the wondrous beauty of the pitch-dark sky.

Trees enveloped in a black canopy,
Stand a mute spectator to my emotions.
I can feel the leaves whispering to me.
The boughs hang down, in
Order to fondle me with their loving arms.

Houses look like ghostly buildings,
Which hold tales of endless horror
Perhaps and never cease to contain
All of life's secret conundrums.

The deserted road seems to enjoy
Moments of calm and repose.
The honking cars continue to
Disturb its tranquility sometimes.

I gaze with awe at these
Sentinels of night as they instill
In me a poetic urge
To write this oeuvre today.

2. *Legacy of Dreams*

While loafing about in my padded chair
I often flip through the pages of a book
I love reading and get lost in the
Vast world of myriad characters and protagonists.

I cry with them; I laugh with them.
My heart empathizes with their joy and pain.
I often forget my own identity and
Drown in a make-believe world of dreams.

I sway in the turbulent sea of emotions-
Sometimes with happiness, at times with sorrow.
I try in vain to grab the fleeting images
Of my favorite characters; their legacy goes on.

3. *Queen of Vice*

Hail, Queen of Vice!
A paragon of sin,
Your eyes speak wrath.
Your face though beautiful
Is a shadow of crime.

Your lips blue from drinking poison
Of the vile acts of dastardly men,
Who have stabbed your once puerile heart
With incessant ruthlessness and
Inflicted upon you immense pain.

You writhe with extreme anguish,
For you know that your innocence
Was misused by nefarious men
To satisfy their insatiable lust,
Thus making a victim of their desire.

Your pretty face is stern.
You stick to a spiteful life
Of vengeance and fury.
You wait for the final showdown
And come out with flying colours.

4. Marvels of God

As dawn arrives, the canvas of the sky
Is tinted with hues of rosy pink.
As if smeared by a paint brush, Nature
Revels in that exquisite art.

Mellow sunshine peeps through the trees to
Reveal the velvety greenery, laden with dew.
I sit in the garden on a chair to
Behold with amazement, the marvels of God.

I become transfixed as I gaze at the wonders
Of the world, only to be mesmerized again and again.
I wonder at all the little perfections in this
Otherwise imperfect world, that are truly awe-inspiring.

5. Cadavers

From the epicentre of tumultuous emotions
Erupts an avalanche of deep-rooted sorrow.
Well-bred and nourished by: utter negligence,
Apathy, disdain, truculence and blithering lies.

What do we do in this make-believe world
Full of deceit, lies and unscrupulousness?
These have been accelerating their pace since
The dawn of civilization, and now spring like volcanoes.

Life loses its literal meaning in this world
Of truculence and mutual animosity.
It's better to die than to live in this fake earth
On which demon-like monsters reside.

Skullduggery has etched in our innocent hearts,
We no longer have faith in the impostors.
We despise this cursed life of vices sucking
Its vitality continually, making it a drab and dry one.

The masks of evil men beguile and confound us.
False promises and true lies repeatedly break our hearts.
Like withered buds, our life is without the basic sap.
Deep agony torches us and we lose hope.

The skulls of skeletons do not haunt us now
As we have faced real apparitions in human-like forms,
In this life of sheer infamy and countless nightmares.
We are just living corpses whose days are numbered.

Like a sprightly nightmare this life rots and dreads us;
Murders our guileless souls with unstoppable treachery.
Lively phantoms of misdeeds and nefariousness wreck us;
In vain, we attempt to extirpate the weeds of piled sin.

6. *Ehereal*

While she listened to the lilting music
Her mind soared above to obscure thoughts:
Cloaked in the cobwebs of fancy,
Snuggling in the pupa of her long-cherished dreams.

She mulled over her sepulchral past;
Exhumed her memories from the cave of her mind,
Bowed her head in indignation over her ill-fate
And the mayhem that had been thrust into her life.

Slowly her plethora of gloom subsided
As the melodious notes lifted her dismal mood.
The ethereal rhapsody captured her subdued heart,
Effaced her pall of gloom with an aura of optimism.

7. *Phantasmagoria*

Abstruse, magical
Images flow in my mind,
Making me happy.

My spirits soar high.
I live, surrounded by dreams:
Fluid, phantom like.

Sometimes I wonder.
Is this real or is this my
Hallucination?

8. *Silver Hope*

Fountains spring from back of the moon.
A beauty- argent, limpid streams:
Blesses my empty heart with boon.

Tendrils entwine the inky sky:
Of beams that sparkle, glitter, shine.
Afloat in heady dreams held high,
A grace remains forever mine.

Tender light caresses my soul,
And wipes my sombre mood wholly.
Glimmering light quenches my whole.

The jewel surfaced canvas shines
At night, through holes peeping behind
The fleecy, candy clouds - and glows
With rays that bore my gloom and grind.

9. Rain Bash

Dark, grey, cumulonimbus clouds afloat
In the lake of the dull sky like a boat.
Billowy, fleecy, flocculent clouds peep
From the drab, grey lacunae inside deep.
Strong, cold gusts rattle the feeble branches
Of my shrubs, and then abrupt rain gushes.
Soaked in rain, the green plants bespeak verdure.
Moist with beads of water, velvety sheen lure.
Deep- pink bougainvilleas fully drenched,
Invite tales of beauty and lust unquenched.
In puddles, children squeal with fun and splash.
Rain splatters, streams down like a birthday bash.
The wet Nature now presents loveliness,
Forms an emotion of togetherness.
The divine charm brings celestial joy,
A bliss, puerile - that no one can destroy.
The bedaubed flora of extreme beauty,
Savours this lonely heart of mine plenty.
A pretty feast for the eyes they present.
An aura of happiness they beget.
Toying with this delicate elegance,
Is a ludicrous act of sheer nonsense.
"Pay homage to this divine creation,
A sculpted pulchritude of perfection."
The smooth leaves frame a glossy greenery,
Of vivid colors form a scenery.

10. Anticipation

Time will arrive again, unfair
Events will vanish and good days will come.
You will forget your scary canvas where
Dark pictures of your battered soul cause
Misgivings of the sunny days and glum
Thoughts, tension always wreck your puerile mind.
Inside your heart remains a wound: become
Decayed with years of careless strokes, unkind
Sweeps of neglect ; that ruin your heart, shred, tear
To pieces; leaving it abandoned, bare.

11. The strange place

I look for a life boat, a log to hold on.
It is my only chance to survive in this whirlpool.
I find no one, sea gulls ply by; waves crash ashore.
Certain of being drowned in the currents, I give up.

Whoa! I am sitting on a horse amidst the whirling sea.
With awe I look at its scaly hindquarter.
Suddenly it flaps its silver-colored wings.
Riding on the argent wings I soar high above the turbulent sea.

It zips past me; I barely can catch my breath.
I hold tightly to its head, afraid of falling down.
Charioted by it, I finally land into a place;
I have never seen before, a field of lush greenery.

There lie juicy, red apples in silver boughs.
I hesitate a bit, but my burning hunger
Impels me to eat those tempting fruits.
Their taste savours and refreshes my taste-buds.

I look here and there with amazement,
Into the strange place I have trodden.
Where is that charioteer, that unique horse?
Eyes scour for him, but in utter futility.

Wearily I sit on the oak bench amidst the dark forest.
A little, pretty girl comes to me and says "Hello."
I reply back and wave smilingly at her.
I find a kind of solace in this absolutely queer land.

She asks me whether I am thirsty.
I immediately express my wish to drink.
She brings a golden glass after a while.
I drink the water and feel revitalized.

Unable to quell my curiosity I ask her name.
She does not reply and remains standstill.
A flitting butterfly comes out of nowhere
And sits on the lass's smooth, silky fingers.

"Boon is my name," says the girl.
Bewildered, I glance at both of them.
" You need not worry," consoles the girl.
Confounded still, I sit: eyes riveted at them.

I ask 'Boon' how I entered this quaint place,
She replies, " Penchant has driven you here."
With a little quiver, I ask her the reason.
"All your wishes will be fulfilled."

Profound excitement fills me as I loiter about.
'Penchant' What a wonderful name I think!
Yells of my Mom " You lazybones !" I hear now.
Awakening from my deep sleep, I realize my dream.

12. Detestable

Uneasy lies my soul, longs for an afterlife.
I rot in darkness, in sheer vice.
Gnashes, moans, whines of this
living apparition reach to deaf ears.

My wrinkled skin, emaciated fingers, outgrown nails:
A despicable appearance of a skeleton,
Frightens all; nobody loves me.
This appalling form, I detest.

The musty odour I emanate
Expels everybody , I cry.
Simmering with rage, I goggle
at the beautiful human beings.

My world has no sunshine, no light.
It is a world that joy is afraid to enter:
A world full of agony,
A world that is cursed, painful.

Is that a ray of light that see?
Or is it my utter caprice?
No, the light now percolates
The darkest crevices of my heart.

A lovely butterfly flits here and there.
A brilliant incidence of luminance
Now enlightens my inglorious world,
Her warmth decreases my dolefulness.

My only companion in this lonely world,
I welcome her whole-heartedly.
An aura of hope, a ray of friendliness;
In this world of insurmountable blackness.

13. *My mind*

Freedom shackled against volition,
against will, against desire, against wish,
against a vortex of suppressed emotions.

Agonized by the chains,
freedom suffers and wrangles,
experiences and feels the condign pain.

Freedom struggles to break free,
strives hard to unfurl itself,
from the fetters of sorrow.

The imprisoned joy wails and howls,
leaves open wounds in the heart
that continue to bleed continually, profusely.

Despair and happiness battle
A fray -violent, riotous and wild
Enough, to penetrate the darkest caverns
Of my mind and perturb them.

14. Dawn

I amble along as the morning star
Unfurls an aura of pale, amber light.
Floating in the lake of dim, blue sky; the
Bits of tiny clouds waft through the mellow
Beams of the partial moon; unwilling to
Shed it's limelight and preens herself in
The mirror of the pallid, azure sky.

The sun rises ushering in a new
Day, to mark in the daily calendar
Of my life, a start; to begin afresh.
Bougainvilleas and chrysanthemums
Adorn my garden with their splendid
Array, an exquisite beauty to rollick
With all my spirits and savour fully.

A cool zephyr embraces my body,
Appeasing me with a serene repose.
A couple of pigeons playfully
Peck at each others' beaks, toying in a
Sprightly manner that fills me with a spirit
So invigorating, enlivening.

A pair of martins nestle on the roof.
I watch the cerulean sky above,
The flight of the birds in a specific
Pattern with their wings fluttering ; as if
To wish me a ' Good Morning' ,making
Me feel revivified with a freshness.

The hues of the dawn shade the canvas of
The sky with pastels of vibrant colours.
Nature's portrait presents a divine charm,
An exquisite pulchritude to make all
The artists zealous to bring forward their
Sheets, to paint using their colour palettes.

I drink in the fresh air and respire with
A vigour, energizing me again.
Agile and nimble as a lamb, I frisk
About in my garden- full of flowers
Of myriad, vivid coloured petals:
That only presents a flawless beauty.

15. *Salvation*

The only vitality in this
moribund life comes from You.
I wish I could grovel at your
Holy Feet and pour all my sins,
For you to wash away with your
Umpteen tears of divine compassion.
I wish I could lie in your Holy
Lap and summon your Holy Grace forever.

Like the hibiscus flower which sweeps
Your Holy Feet, I want a salvation.
I want a liberation from the worldly
desires that fetter me incessantly.
I am groping for a speck of
light, a ray of hope in this
pit of abysmal darkness that
seems to drown me with its grisly beck.

16.   *Phantoms of Past*

The phantoms of her past continue
To haunt her and wreck her life fully.
She tries hard to expel the spooks of her
Mind but they mangle her again and again.

She cowers in terror of the ghastly images
That run across the canvas of her psyche.
She often experiences hallucinations,
And tries in vain to grab her fleeting thoughts.

She fails to live in her present as
Her brain is preoccupied by the demons
Which like heavy blizzards in winter,
Continue to wreak havoc on the turf of her soul.

17. Disaster

I still cannot wake up
From that disaster
In my life when I lost
My soul-mate, my mother forever.

It is an ill-starred event
That I cannot forgo, rather
I love to exhume the last
Vestiges of her presence in my soul.

I feel her love throbbing
In my veins, coursing through
My whole body today but
Will feel the same in future.

It is not that I am excavating
Memories of her existence, now considered flimsy;
But it is her utmost heady love potion
That I am actually drunk by.

18. *Down the Memory Lane*

In my quest for an
Independence, a liberation
From the living nightmare
That I am bound in; I often
Mull over the extreme happiness
I had in the prime of my life.

Memories stream down to the summertime,
When I watered my garden
With sprinklers during the evening,
And the aroma of wet grass pervaded
My nostrils, making me feel
Refreshed and invigorated.

I remember those halcyon days
When I used to have a gala time
During the celebration of my birthdays
With family and friends and gorge
The sumptuous chicken grilled
On the barbecue and feel ecstatic.

Gone are those days when
My grandchildren used to
Play with crackers and fireworks
And illuminate my life with
An aura of profound joy,
Bliss, satisfaction and fulfillment.

I am now battling an incurable
Disease in this old age with
No one to care for me or give
Support in times of utmost need.
I am absolutely alone in this world
With no one to empathize my sorrow.

19. Dragon lore

Once upon a time there lived a dragon,
In a dank cave, on an island barren.
He was brutal in nature, and used to
Breathe fire; damage lives that none could undo.

Onto there, a saint placed his pure footsteps;
Ushering a new dawn at his doorsteps.
He gave the old critter a golden coin.
From his vices, his soul, he did disjoin.

As time passed, he became more innocent.
As sunrise peeped, his sins became absent.
Drowned by a vortex of virtues, he changed.
As the New Year came, his life, rearranged.

20. Demons of mind

She saw a missed call on her phone
But her gloomy mood prevailed and
She did not pick it up to see
The caller, to avoid people.

Buried in her brooding distress:
She had lost interaction with
The ones whom she loved once deeply.
Her contact with the world had severed.

She recalled the time spent in a
Cafe which once was her hangout.
But the pall of gloom swathed her
In a cell of abject darkness.

She had been battling her demons
Of her mind for quite a long time,
But the devils lurked and posed a
Threat to her flimsy existence.

21. Supplication

Sitting at the backyard, my mind hovers
Through a barque that unloads past memories
Of fun, frolic and laughter with my family.

Oh! How I yearn for those jubilant days
Which bloomed like the flowers in spring and
Suffused the air with the smell of freshly cut grass.

As I stretch out my calloused hands,
I find no one to support me in
This deplorable solitude and rotting senility.

Alas! I beseech in vain to find only tears
As my true companion in this sheer distress.
Nature stands a mute spectator to my sorrow.

Did I forget that immortal power of love
That transcends all the barriers of hostility
And spreads its wings and ameliorates my pain?

I suddenly feel joyous and smile as I feel
For His Holy raft that sails me smoothly
By this turbulent ocean of agony to utter bliss.

22. Karma and Life

Life is not always for frolic and fun.
Sometimes we have to walk and sometimes run.
There are ups, downs- it never stops flowing.
It moves and turns on like a stone rolling.

To where it will halt we surely don't know.
By our deeds, the seeds we shall sow.
Then reap the recompense of our actions.
Our Karma will decide our reactions.

Good work gets rewarded as our delight.
Gladness fills us after doing things right.
Misdeeds end up in sorrow, affliction;
That's why we often face tribulation.

23. *Apocalypse*

When gloom aggravates,
Ghostly shadows of evil chase;
We sink and bemoan.

We grope for a new
hope but often in vain we
fumble and flounder.

Bright revelation
titillates and scintillates.
Aura of new hope.

Olive branches crack
Open and entwine themselves
Like flocking doves.

Mind elevated
to a noble, sublime peak
Now transpires.

24. Black hole

She wept incessantly,
Strived hard to bury her memories
In the deepest black holes of her mind
Where no luminance penetrates.

She idled the hours in melancholy,
"An agonized soul, is she, "everyone says.
No optimistic whim enters her darkest
Black holes lurking in the caves of her mind.

She counts her days in vain and pledges
That her grim existence is limited.
She confesses before The Almighty
To terminate her wasted, brittle life.

Her emotions are bird-caged in the
Vortex of miseries, she humbly pleads
To God to mend her morose black holes;
To recompense for her vile misdeeds.

A sudden lightning flashes in the dark
Sky of her utterly black mind, erases her
Deep-rooted despondence, shatters her black holes.
And radiance shines within, whittling down her black holes.

25. Falls

The dull monotony frets her.
Drab, outlandish landscapes fetter.
Out of the rustic land ,she retreats.
Charm of the rolling rapids ,she meets.

She muses on her treachery.
Her cheeks turn ruby with fury.
The stream amidst the ranges calms,
A gentle woman she becomes.

She now forgets to take revenge,
The soothing grace dissolves her rage.
The serene pulchritude pleases,
Divine elegance appeases.

26. A butterfly

Bright, gossamer wings
Flit from flower to flower.
Queen of the garden!

27. *Bucolic Beauty*

As dawn breaks ,the sun scatters its scarlet light.
It ushers the beginning of a new day.
The sleepy farm wakes up with spirits new, bright.
The sun peeps through the fleecy, white clouds hung tight.
Darkness of the night is dispelled right away.
As dawn breaks the sun scatters its scarlet light.
Farmers ready to set their daily chores right,
With trucks and tractors they begin their workday.
The sleepy farm wakes with spirits new, bright.
Slowly the sky is suffused with amber light.
I wonder at Nature's colourful display.
As the dawn breaks, the sun scatters its scarlet light.
Pigs in the pen oink and have a noisy fight.
From a big haymow, a hungry cow eats hay.
The sleepy farm wakes up with spirits new, bright.
Such a pleasure to behold the rural sight!
The simple beauty of the farm makes me gay.
As dawn breaks the sun scatters its scarlet light.
The sleepy farm wakes up with spirits new, bright.

28. Vacation

Vibrant moments whiled away:
An enjoyment spiced with hot
Coffee and fresh, yummy cookies.
Ambling with the dear ones-spending
Time plentiful, of laughter and tears.
In memory's box it will be stored,
Opened only when I am sad; And
Nurtured with love, affection.

29. *This Broken Heart*

Till this day I remember,
How you had used my
Innocent love towards you and
Shredded it to pieces.

Blind in love with you,
Renouncing my self for you, I
Offered you my utmost devotion.
Knowing not the consequences, I
Earnestly loved you and wanted to
Nestle myself in your heart.

How stupid I have been!
Entrusting my heart to you ,
A great blunder; it has been.
Revenge is what I now need,
To recover from my mangled heart.

30. *Vale of tears*

I always dreamt of going with
You to a valley of rainbows:
Where the colours of our love would
Outshine my black and white world
Full of pain, sorrow, agony.

I always dreamt of going with
You to a valley of rain,
Where my motley dreams would come true.
There our love would effloresce
Like the multicoloured flowers.

But you turned my life into a
Vale of tears by unfaithfulness,
Insincerity, betrayal.
You snubbed me and led me to the
Slaughter of my innocent dreams.

31. *The Gateway to Heaven*

Folded hands in orison,
To terminate the evil
Predators of today's world.
Political wars and bloodbaths-
Jabbing into the hearts of
Innocent civilians,
Gnawing at their delicate
Flesh, steeping them in pools
Of blood surely usher in
"A door to Hell" unbidden,
Unpremeditated,
Unpalatable and
Unhallowed. The firing
Of cannon balls, the outburst
Of expletives and bombshells,
For usurpation of
Money, power and position;
Racking the whole world need to
Be stopped permanently
And be the harbinger
Of peace, love and happiness,
"The Gateway to Heaven."

32. Music

Mellifluous notes vibrate.
Usher a realm of magic.
Soothe my agony and pain.
Ignite my passion to sing.
Complete me, make me whole.

33.   *A Star to Guide Me*

I stare at the zillion stars
Studding the black, velvety night sky
And wonder which among them is
A star to guide me and support
Me; like a mother protects her
Child and steers him to safety.

I find my answer in Your grace
And blessings, showered from above.
You are the brightest star that glows
And illuminates my dark world
With the light of your compassion,
Love, affection and forgiveness.

A star to guide me, you sparkle
In my life when things go amiss.
A star to guide me, you are there
When I am saddled with problems;
To lighten my load and resolve them.

A star to guide me, in times of
Difficulty when no one
Is there to share my affliction.
A star to guide me, when I do
Something wrong and repent for it.
A star to guide me, I feel your
Presence in everything I do.

34. *Where are You, Christmas Angels?*

Where are You, Christmas Angels?
When innocent babies die
Due to undernourishment,
Unroofed children shiver in
Intense cold, struggle to live.
When lascivious men assault
A girl, kill her womanhood,
Shatter her bright, puerile dreams.
When bed-ridden people at their
Deaths' doors writhe with agony,
Finally succumb to the
Greedy jaws of death and find
Peace and joy forever.

Are you there for them to stretch
Your helping hand, guide them with
The light of your love and care,
Or will you abandon them
In their acute suffering?

35.   *An ode to Keats*

Of redbreasts and larks he dreams;
He pens poems and daydreams.
Tears of the past effaced,
My sorrow and gloom; he erased.

Through his eyes Nature seems calm,
Serene beauty turns a balm;
Wipes out my sheer despondence;
Fills me with bliss, happiness.

Splendid rhymes form symphonies,
To all sorts of melodies.
Poets compose eulogies,
I sing with euphonies.

But joy is not always life,
Which Keats showed in extreme strife.
Battling with an ailing health,
He succumbed to a black death.

His legacy will remain.
Magical words will sustain
Bards to write encomium.
I sing with harmonium.

36. *Life's book*

Letters leap out of the pages.
Tossed by the winds, twigs scatter here.
Creases of the old book usher
An age marked by negligence.

From the white leaves of the Life's book
Letters leap out of the pages.
Old age now romps with complete win.
Youth, spring; now totally deceased.

The once fountain named Life now springs
From the dilapidated life's book.
Letters leap out of the pages.
Dried sprigs now gather, amass here.

In the battle of Life youth dies.
For a loving rapport, heart cries.
From the encumbered , old ages.
Letters leap out of the pages.

37. *Raindrops*

As I watch the raindrops pelting down my
Window panes, my thoughts wander away, hover.
I think of the unique creation weaved
By God through His magical fingers that
Wash my despondence, gloom, dolefulness and
Make my spirits soar high above smoothly.

Smaller droplets coalesce into bigger
Ones , forming a uniform stream of rain.
Just like past moments turning away to
The present and then to the future, thus
Creating a continuous flow of
Water: pure and pristine in its form.

38. Doldrums

I pine for those halcyon days,
When I used to be happy without
Any condition or restraint.

I pine for those halcyon days,
When I used to be carefree and
Happy-go-lucky without any problem.

I pine for those halcyon days,
When I used to laugh heartily
And sorrow retreated.

I pine for those halcyon days,
When I was not encumbered
With grave responsibilities.

I pine for those halcyon days,
When joy was aplenty and
Limitless like the flowers in spring.

I pine for those halcyon days,
When mirth was abundant and
So strong; sorrow dreaded to enter.

39. To my student

I cannot forgive you for your mistakes.
You have committed them again and again.
I know you have the right resourcefulness.
Why don't you just give it a hard battle ?
You will see that everything will be fine.
Don't vacillate or delay, you must act.

I know; you are in a stressed position.
But you must try to learn from your mistakes.
For you, this stress is not desirable.
You must try to overcome and attempt.
Give it an honest, zealous and hard try.
Things will spontaneously become good.

Don't think that others are better than you.
Shun this sheer pessimistic attitude.
Nothing in this world is impossible.
Everyone at some point of life does wrong.
But resilient human beings survive.
Think positive, then only you can calm.

In this life things always don't go correct.
In times of strife you must learn to resume.
Don't give up, success will pursue again.
Positive thinking will keep you going.
Only wise men learn from their past mistakes.
The essence is that they honestly try.

There is no option to this, you must try.
You will find that this is the best method.

But don't get bogged down by paltry mistakes,
Then things will never turn good and outdo.
You must listen carefully to my words.
Otherwise failure will prevail over.

I have a belief that you will succeed.
I know, you are going to try with zeal.
You are pondering over my words now.
Those days are not far, when things will go right.
You will then automatically feel good.
I know, in future you will not fail.

If you don't act now, you will commit wrong
Again in future like unlearned lessons.
Only fools repeat their mistakes again.
Life is a struggle, you must persevere.

40. *New Moon*

It is time to shed not a tear,
For finally here is New Year.
To forget all the past throes
Is now life's motto: no more woes.

To laugh heartily till life's end,
Previous sorrow now to rend;
Has become my life's new keyword,
I will chirp gladly like a bird.

I know that life is to mingle
Joy and anguish that are ample.
I will focus on the new moon
That is about to come very soon.

41. *Rainy day*

Parched lips of the earth move slightly
As drops of rain pelt down.
The once dry soil now quenches its
Thirst by drinking ample water.

Moist leaves glisten with fallen drops,
Create a magical view of
Nature with its lush greenery
And the lovely scent of the rain.

42. Old love

Humming birds
sing songs in the orchards:
melodies that touch my broken heart.

Memories from the past appear and tear apart
my soul with painful feelings that never depart.

Flames of my long-lost love resurface;
that I cannot erase,
my old craze.

43. Mask

Often demons lurk
Behind the masked complaisance
Of human beings.

It's hard to fathom
Their real innermost feelings,
Within this disguise.

44. *Sun versus Moon*

The fiery ball shines brilliantly,
An aura of scintillating radiance permeates.

Its robust shine glares at me
Like an arrogant, haughty person.
I do refute its superciliousness;
The domineering attitude invokes hatred.

I cherish the night star gleaming
With a splendid smile, it gazes at me.
Playing hide and seek with the flocculent clouds;
It waves at me amiably and heartily.

Its lovely, inviting face laughs at me merrily,
Thus soothing and appeasing my frayed nerves.
I wake up every morning with dreamy eyes
That burn brightly to ashes,
Only to rekindle my fancies
In the absolute stillness of night.

45. *Vitality*

Mellow sunshine
Unfolds itself.
A sunflower
Efflorescent,
Is a picture
Of sprightliness;
Energizing
Myself anew.

46. *Insight*

There lived a pretty girl who dreamt
Lovely fancies, those did her tempt.
To an unknown world dazzling, kempt;
Landed she, emptiness undreamt.
To escape, she made an attempt.
Ludicrous whims met with contempt.
Tears rolling, she did pre-empt
Loads of wild notions she once dreamt.

47. Mirages

While sloshing through the puddles
With rubber boots after rain occurred,
I watched a child drifting away a paper
Boat with full of merriment and fun.

My mind hovered back to my childhood,
Where I used to watch a duck waddling.
Those halcyon days of rainbow dreams
Are now but mere mirages in my mind.

48. *Morning glory*

The morning sun fills the canvas of the
Sky with flowing colours of orange and
Red, as if painted by a brush.
It brings those dead emotions
Alive on once blank easel
Which now holds a vibrant picture.

Fluffy clouds playing a peek-a-boo with
The sun, create a magical game of
Light and darkness.
My mind wanders freely
In the misty lair formed
By those flocculent, billowy, white puffs.

Oblivious of the past gloom, I now
Enter a realm of celestial bliss.
I stare in awe at the splendid beauty
Of Nature as it unfolds itself with
Vivid hues of scarlet and tangerine.
An aura of bliss enwreathes me.

49. *Mobile pattern*

Shells drift ashore like
Content flitting from flower
To flower, changeable.

Mirth and sorrow come
Alternately to form an
Ever-changing life cycle.

50. *Volition*

I
Have dreamed
Of scaling
Heights where no one
Can reach, the zenith;
But will my goal be met
With this weak attitude of
Mine that crumbles under hurdles
Like a pack of cards, and wrenches hard
Like a helpless captive struggling to flee?

For that I need perseverance, strong will;
That will break through even the iron
Walls of depression and sorrow.
Become strong and overcome
All the impediments.
I have to conquer
My feebleness and
Weak psyche to
Work hard,
Try.

51. *Grief and Dolefulness*

Doling out woe.
Doling out grief.
Grief stricken mind.
Grief wrapped psyche.
Psyche longs for mirth.
Psyche craves for bliss.
Bliss laden days.
Bliss sheathed past.
Past is ample joy.
Past is vibrant dreams.
Dreams, now skulk.
Dreams, now sink.
Sinking in gloom.
Sinking in despair.
Despair begets sloth.
Despair procures pain.
Pain creates tension.
Pain makes me sad.
Sad thoughts engender
Sad feelings, despondence.
Despondent lives lurk in
Despondent houses.
Houses, full of ghosts.
Houses, swarmed with phantoms.
Phantoms lurk inside.
Phantoms appal.
Appalling house bewails.
Appalling abode cries.
Cries of skeletal remains

Cries of wretched presence.
Presence once dwelt.
Presence always lived.
Lived a dream of 'Life',
Lived a dream of gaiety.
Gaiety once stayed here.
Gaiety flourished here.
Here, no frolic dwells.
Here, no fun lingers.
Lingers only ample woe.
Lingers only gloom.
Gloom prevails.
Gloom persists here.
Here, no life remains.
Here, only darkness stays.
Staying in a coffin.
Staying in a graveyard.
Graveyard- macabre and grim.
Graveyard- gruesome, awful.
Awful dolefulness.
Awful dolefulness.
Dolefulness suffocates.
Dolefulness torments.
Torments.
Suffocates.

52. Trials of Life

Often life becomes perilous.
Obfuscated, we stop, falter.
Overloaded with stress, nervous-
Overwhelmed, tense in our danger.

Fear grapples us with all its might.
Fumbling, we don't know what to do.
Fortitude is what we need right.
Forbearance can be our rescue.

Easily we can overcome
Every obstacle in our life,
Each thorn in our path if become
Equable even in our strife.

As we face each hurdle with ease
And thread our way through the risky
Acclivities, worrying we cease.
At last our spirits turn lively.

53. *Paradise*

Distraught with this world of complexities,
I started brooding over this helpless
Condition of mine; struggling alike a
Prisoner trapped in this desolate earth.

Wearied down by the dull monotony,
I fell asleep and dreamed of a lovely
Place with lush green meadows, and a gentle
Breeze fondling my body with light touches.

I looked at the azure sky above, with
The white fleecy clouds peeping from outside.
Suddenly a vibrant rainbow flashed out,
And I saw beautiful Angels smiling
At me and blessing me from The Heaven;
As if I were in a paradise.

My cell rang and with sleepy eyes, I,
Picked it up going back to my true life.

54. *Solitude*

Do you remember that vine?
That witnessed our pristine love.
I wish you were only mine,
Cooing peace like a dove.

Blue tits singing with mirth,
Remind me of my old love.
Sweet memories I unearth,
Cooing peace like a dove.

This broken heart of despair
Bleeds with my wounded love.
I seek solace in my lair,
Cooing peace like a dove.

My heart bespeaks loneliness
Of a pure, guileless love.
I crave for joy, happiness;
Cooing peace like a dove.

I never can forget you.
How could you dump my love?
This lone heart is born anew,
Cooing peace like a dove.

55. *The Yeti*

Amidst the snow-capped mountains lives a vile
Looking dragon named 'Yeti', with its sheer
Gloom enveloping the whole icy cave:
Reeking of a musty odour; ghoulish.

She lives in an abundant land- full of
Apricots and luscious peaches throbbing
With vivaciousness, ample sprightliness.
She flails her hands in the air with immense joy.

She is sitting alone on a chair in her room,
When suddenly a black silhouette frightens
Her and she, losing control of mind;
Screams and raves wildly like a lunatic.

The abominable Yeti pounces
Upon her, and tugs at her clothes in order
To exhibit its utter shamelessness.
Poses an unfathomable ruthlessness.

She roars and screeches after being stabbed
By the beast, and begs for the only alms
Of her own very existence, and she
Is filled with tremendous terror, panic.

A sprinkle of exquisite flowers from
Above jolts her, she gropes for a new
Horizon in her life; as her mirth sways
Away her past sorrow, and she rollicks.

The Yeti weeps now tears of penitence.
In solitude and loneliness, pass his
Days of pure gloom and uncanny remorse;
And it bangs its head at the willow tree.

The Yeti now speaks his deeds of mistakes,
In a crowd thronging with thousands of people.
The Yeti now shakes hands with his victim,
Pleads humbly saying that, "I am sorry."

56. *Hues*

I goggle at the cerulean sky ;
Its vibrant, bright colour makes me high.
Lolling on the beach, I gaze at the sea
Breaking white foam ashore with ample glee.

The seagulls soar and flutter in gaiety.
I gawk at the charming, pleasant beauty.
Nature presents subtle loveliness
With utmost charm and readiness.

An array of hues it presents.
A divine grace it represents.
An aura of heavenly bliss
Fills me as the cool zephyrs kiss.

57. *Sultry dreams*

Her parched lips crave for more water.
Scorching rays scald and torment her.
Just a little sip now she needs.
Sweat on her forehead forms in beads.
Her delicate skin cracks endure
The sultry season without cure.
For rainfall she wants to wait.
A downpour she wishes to create.
She will drink from the lovely spring
Joy welling up, mirth it will bring.
Alas! Her sultry dreams decease.
The fiery ball rises with ease.

58. *Veneration*

Oh Lord! Save your children from their sins,
Who murder guileless souls and drink gins.

In this world filled with sheer treachery,
Breach of faith is a pure mockery.

Gone are those days filled with pure gaiety,
Thrives in the hearts only cruelty.

I offer you my abysmal pain,
Everyone is obsessed with their gain.

Where are those blue larks that used to sing?
An aura of calm they used to bring.

Ravaging wars fill us with turmoil.
In turbulence, ourselves, we embroil.

I present You this holy lotus,
To battle our wrecked lives and bless us.

I place this faith on your sacred shrine,
For a celestial light to shine.

59. *Last request*

She held herself tightly to her bosom with ardent passion.
Tears trickling down her pretty face, make a living corpse.
Hope buried in the macabre grave of animate beings,
To portend a doom that is invincible and grisly.

She now remains a cadaver of her past sweet memories.
Long lost in the sea waves lashing upon the shore, and spreading
Sand-particles and pebbles with an unbridled frenzy of rage;
Sweeping off the once foamy, gentle ripples in abyss.

His mighty hands grabbed her so tightly that she tried hard to
Wrench from the writhing pain and deepest agony: entwining
Her to a pall of dismal despondence, enshrouding her;
With a bouquet of innumerable black roses smiling.

Black roses wave at her and welcome her with open hands.
They entice her to a kingdom full of darkness, a sheet
Of utter blackness; a canopy of sheer despair that
Happiness is afraid to enter or amble in front.

Her body limps from the incurable disease that sucks
Her life-blood and guzzles her life-drink, thus enfeebling her.
She makes a last attempt to 'live once again' as He strides with
A fast pace toward her, ushering her to that cradle.

A heavy sigh she heaves as her head drops and her body
Slouches in an imbalanced way: as she waddles with small,
Light steps to that ultimate, deadly, final destination.
She pauses for a while but has nothing to turn back on.

60. *The Philosophy of Life*

Joy and sorrow hold their hands together
As we pass through a cycle eternal.
Life can be sharp thorns but not forever.
Mirth and pain stay but not perpetual.

"Life is not a bed of roses," we say.
But as we reach at its termination:
Our mistakes we find; the causes that lie
Behind; we learn without definition.

Flowers of bright colours in life's bouquet
Wither, but their fragrance never erase…
The happiness stored in the mere casket
Of sweet memories, never we efface.

Of guilt and misdeeds we never repent,
A new conscience unfurls; lessons beget.

61. Apple of her eye

She pressed her child closely to her breast
To keep dangerous risks and strifes at bay.
Amid her loving lap the small girl lay,
Nestling with peace with her mother in rest.
Many sleepless nights passed by in unrest,
Of her mom to protect her child away
From the deep anxiety that used to fray
Her nerves, an endless love at her bequest.

To nourish her child, none can be better.
Her love, blood and soul throb through her veins.
A loyal, staunch bond they form together.
In her mom's nest, she remains.
Embedded in her heart, she lies ; whether
Anyone cares or not, shares, feels or gains.

62. Imagination

Fierce sun torches me, I suffer.
Extreme thirst fills me with anger.
I wish I could roam about in
A bower and rest in an inn.

Heat stings me with brutal rashes,
With frustration teeth gnashes.
I feel like roasted in a furnace;
Severe perspiration, no less.

Crawling on the wings of fancy,
To a quaint place I wish to flee.
A land where birds chirp and twitter.
Pervades the air, perfume of myrrh.

I will gorge the juicy berries
Of myrtle and watch the birdies,
Hovering above me with glee.
Their freedom shackled by no key.

Gallons of fresh water I drink,
Vortices of misery sink.
Rejuvenated and refreshed,
Ample happiness felt, enmeshed.

Ouch! I look at the red pimple,
Burning like that sun in April.
Vanishes imagination,
Heads towards true destination.

63. *A little girl's dream*

Once there lived a pretty small girl
Whose stepmother was but a churl.
Her black hair was smooth as satin.
She had a beautiful fair skin.
Her stepmother was envious
And her actions were villainous.
One day she gave her an orange
Which was of a colour bit strange.
A doubt struck her and she threw it.
Hurling the orange in a pit.
The witch stepmother came to know
And she wanted a deadly show.
So she cooked a poisonous broth
Which was sizzling and full of froth.
She served it with a spatula.
She hunted her like a cheetah.
All her wild attempts fizzled out
When suspicion made Alice flout.
Pouring it under a willow tree,
The clever girl wanted to flee.
She followed a footprint and ran
And a new adventure began.
At night she found a dark, queer cave
From which a music made her rave.
A group of elves resided there.
Her joy and pain they used to share.
One day a handsome prince arrived.
All her glee he gladly revived.

He took her in a trolley car,
She lived like the wife of a Czar.

64. Lutes

Rustic dreams turn pastoral
As they wander through landscapes,
Of greenery usual .
Lutes of the bard create waves.

As mind moves through the mazes
Of magnificent dreamscapes,
With joy a fairy bounces,
Lutes of the bard create waves.

Ghosts of my past terrify.
Images in mindscapes
Stand tall, bold and horrify.
Lutes of the bard make waves.

As I flip through the pages
Of romance in bright moonscapes,
Darkness goes; pain effaces.
Lutes of the bard create waves.

65. Dulcet tunes

Mellifluous notes waft through air;
Splitting me from my evil dream.
The cuckoo sings, chirps in its lair.

Tunes resound of a sweetness rare,
With profound ecstasy I beam.
Mellifluous notes waft through air.

With wonder, at the bird I stare.
Morning beams flood the sky and gleam.
The cuckoo sings, chirps in its lair.

Heart filled with joy, beyond compare.
A mere daydream it does not seem.
Mellifluous notes waft through air.

Sorrow effaced, mirth I now bear.
Soothes my soul, the dulcet stream.
The cuckoo sings, chirps in its lair.

Gladly I recite my prayer.
My soul filled with a bliss, extreme.
Mellifluous notes waft through air.
The cuckoo sings, chirps in its lair.

66. My shepherd

The Lord is my shepherd, I lack nothing.
To the Almighty I owe everything.

I never have to think to quench my thirst,
Happy: I feel that I am not accursed.

I know not what are hunger, poverty.
I treat Him with utmost care, loyalty.

Never did I desire for more money,
I feel wholly satisfied and bonny.

I feel for those who do not have shelter,
Aghast at their sorry state, I falter.

I feel blessed that I have a sweet home,
Feel pain for those who lie in streets and roam.

I think of His boons even in sorrow,
For He always brings a new tomorrow.

I think of Him when I feel sad, lonely,
His love is enough to make me happy.

For being His daughter, I take sheer pride.
The rough struggles of life, I put aside.

For what I have, I owe Him gratitude.
To fight hardships- I plead for fortitude.

67. *Exalted*

Shimmering rays percolate through my heart,
Effacing the weeds of yesteryear.

Pristine sunshine glitters in my window,
Embracing me with ample affection.

Day ends with the voluptuous twilight,
Painting the canvas of my soul.

Moonbeams smile at me,
Through the star-studded sky.

Night befalls but the light
Never extinguishes, an aura of mirth
Envelops; and caresses me now.

68. Nature's Picture

Dark grey sky peeping through the lattice of the
Patterned branches forms a mesh, a maze.
Yonder stands a tree with its serrated
Leaves :as if awaiting someone in pangs,
Of abject solitude and despondence.

Twilight is about to set in with hues,
Brilliant, vibrant, vivid and splendid.
Morning glory has vanished with all its
Dazzling brilliance and resplendent sheen,
Leaving behind a trail of utter gloom.

A pall of sheer despair unfolds itself.
Soon darkness will arrive swathing the
Jet black canvas, in wreaths of pristine pain.
The night star gleams at me with a smile
So cherubic , I welcome the pure grace.

The diamond-studded canopy twinkles
Feebly, a portrait of picturesque charm.
Without radiance, without bright luster,
But with a comeliness enticing the
Poets- to doodle for all ages to come.

69. *Charisma*

Sun rays percolating through the glassy splinters
Usher warmth, relief through craggy splinters.

Panorama of the azure sky,
A beauty to cherish through dainty splinters.

Resplendent with the morning glory,
Bitter chill erased through cozy splinters.

Respite from the wintry gusts,
Enticing pleasure through cushy splinters.

The daystar with its mellow beams
Presents a view through the lovely splinters.

70. A woman named Kim

Once, there lived a buxom girl called Kim.
She was pretty who longed to be slim.
She gave birth to one child.
For two, husband did chide.
She became fat and failed to stay trim.

71. Gothic Celebration

Refrain

Bewails of a woman haunt me.
My birthday party is accursed.
Is that a phantom that I see?
Or my vices, that need be purged?

Burst balloons envelop the ink.
Visage of a pallid woman:
Is that a face, I goggle at ?
Or my whims, that I need to ban?

Refrain

Headless apparition appears.
My fun ebbs, laughter disappears.
I shriek and scream in vain despair.
My face becomes smudged with all tears.

The ghost ushers me furtively,
Into the darkest hole I land.
Mysterious cries scare me off.
I sink in the sprinkled, black sand.

Refrain
Grisly terror now grips me with
It's jutting claws and tight fetters.
I try to unbuckle myself
From the shackles of chained jitters.

The creepiest feeling swallows
Me, and I cry relentlessly.
Ebony canopies of pain
Sheathe me , I fight desperately.

Refrain

72. The Cycle of Life

Jingle bells chime, as Santa sets
His reindeer ready for a Merry
Christmas: that will be the harbinger
Of new hope, and filled with laughter.

Streets embellished with grand neon bulbs
gleam, as people mark the beginning
Of a New Year with lots of frolic;
Bidding goodbye to the past year.

As life rolls on we forget the old
And always welcome the new,
Alike memories which change
In the flowing cycle of life.

73. The Sunset of Life

We all head towards eternity-
the ultimate goal of our life;
after we complete our stay
in this transient sphere.
We must be prepared
for the sunset,
as it brings
a new
start.

74. Infamous Glories

Little girl never dream again,
This grim darkness brings only pain.
Bury your splendid memories,
Dissolve in infamous glories.

In this abysmal, inky place;
Deep angst speaks always to debase.
Wishes, luscious like red cherries
Dissolve in infamous glories.

Life is not a bed of roses;
It's full of thorns, prickly poses.
Golden desires in treasuries,
Dissolve in infamous glories.

Little girl never dream again,
Dissolve in infamous glories.

75. Chivalrous

We are mighty women of strong power.
Our magic is rare like a sorcerer.
We are mighty women of strong power.

We are intrepid, we never glower.
We might bleed, gore does not make us cower.
Our magic is rare like a sorcerer.

Our pluck never ebbs, failures empower.
Women of steel: to us, men are lower.
We might bleed, gore does not make us cower.

We have abundant strength like a soldier.
We are strong fighters with mental power.
Women of steel: to us, men are lower.

We are warriors with shining armour.
We shoot arrows like an expert archer.
We are strong fighters with mental power.

To our failures, patience is the answer.
We are mighty women of strong power.
We shoot arrows like an expert archer.
We are mighty women of strong power.

76. Just Dreaming

Yesterday a fairy appeared in my dream,
Who blessed me and gifted me a dream catcher.
I see now a handsome prince riding on a
Stallion , bedecked with silver trinkets, jingling
Like church bells ,posing an auspicious event;
None other than tying my knot with that man.

What a fantastic moment in my life , now filled
With tons of happiness and plentiful fun!
He slipped a platinum ring on my finger,
Held my hand with a firm promise that will
Never die and swathed me with his precious
Love and murmured in my ears words of love.

Morning flooded the sky with brilliant hues
Of red and orange, giving it a bright sheen.
I am now frantically looking for him,
The Man of my dreams and my soulmate who kindled
In me raging flames of passion that will not
Surcease but will only be quenched by his love.

77. Dream Cottage

Come with me, I'll show you a castle,
Where lush fields of greenery nestle
Beneath the vast, cerulean sky;
Holding nice dreams, hopes and wishes high;
Surrounding the beautiful dale.

There lies the sweet home of dreams ample,
Pretty girls with plaited hair amble.
A placid, limpid lake lies nearby.
Come with me.

Flocking with plenty sheep and cattle,
The fields emanate a gay babble,
Which is neither a laugh nor a cry;
Neither a choked tear nor a sad sigh,
But is an abundance of chortle.
Come with me.

78. *Magical Eggs*

A doleful chick was passing by,
Thinking of her wicked friend's lie.
Stunned by a world of make-believe,
She was waiting for a reprieve.

A funny bunny caught her eye,
With a smiling face who said, "Hi."
Surprised, the chick asked "Who are you?"
"Easter Bunny, your friend new."

She said, "I don't want any friend
To wreck me and my heart to rend."
With flopping ears and a cute smile,
He said, "I know this world is vile."

"But true friends are here which are rare,
Your sorrow and joy they will share.
I have lovely eggs up my sleeve
With a new life for you to weave."

79. A Christmas Dream

Humpty Dumpty went to the mall
To buy small Christmas gifts for all.
A nice shawl for his wife he bought,
And for his daughter a cute cot.

He intended to purchase more
But the high prices made him sore.
With a gloomy face he came back.
Doleful, that his money did lack.

80. Enchantment

Behold the lady cloaked in blue
Whose dreamy eyes bespeak a tale
Of passion that bewitches you,
Arises love alike a gale.

The silver ball reflects a light,
A beauty like the starry night.
She warbles dulcet tunes through air,
Creates a charm beyond compare.

81. Freedom

Crystal clouds float in the blue lake,
Above the verdant stretch of grass.
A gentle breeze embraces her,
Lightly stroking her body to
Soothe her frayed nerves, anxiety;
Release her burden of worries,
Vacate the fetters of her mind,
And savour the taste of freedom.